IN THIS ADVENTURE

Bulldozer

Giraffe

The Government Minister

Professor Octavius Shard

The Television Crew

For Mimi, with my love

GUMDROP
AND THE BULLDOZERS

Story and pictures by Val Biro

HODDER AND STOUGHTON
LONDON SYDNEY AUCKLAND TORONTO

OF ALL THE things that Mr Josiah Oldcastle enjoyed in life, driving his car was the thing he liked the best. And no wonder, because his car was a very special vehicle indeed: an Austin Clifton Heavy 12/4, vintage 1926. It was Gumdrop, no less.

So on this fine day he should have been enjoying himself. But he was not, because of all the things he *disliked*, driving on a jam-packed motorway was the worst. And this one was the most crowded and smelliest motorway of all.

At long last they came to their junction and turned off. 'Ah, this is much better,' said Mr Oldcastle, and his dog Horace woofed. They were on their way to stay with Sir Marmaduke Ricketty-Cobwebb at Mildew Manor, to see the wild animals in his Safari Park. Mr Oldcastle looked forward to the peace and quiet of the place.

Suddenly a huge bulldozer emerged from a side road and it would have grabbed Gumdrop in its shovel if Mr Oldcastle had not jammed on the brakes. 'Really, this is too bad!' he growled as the bulldozer trundled ahead, choking them with dust. In any case, what would a bulldozer be doing at Mildew Manor of all places?

When they arrived at the manor, they were welcomed by Sir Marmaduke himself. Usually he was a cheerful man, but now he looked most upset. 'I have bad news,' he said. 'A new motorway has been planned to cut across the far end of my Safari Park. I have been fighting this plan for nearly a year now, but it was no good – work is due to start next Monday. The bulldozers are already in place.'

Mr Oldcastle was appalled to hear this. 'A motorway! We can't have a smelly motorway *here!* What would your animals think?'

At any rate Horace didn't think much of it, and when he started to growl, Mr Oldcastle decided to act. Together with Sir Marmaduke he drew up a plan of action.

First, they got up a petition. The very next morning
Gumdrop and Bunbo the elephant went to the nearby town,
carrying posters. They collected so many signatures that
Bunbo had to hold up the long petition in his trunk.

Sir Marmaduke came along in his Rolls-Royce Silver
Ghost, and his own list was so long that a giraffe had to
carry it in her mouth. People kept signing the petitions, and
by the end of the day there were over a thousand signatures.

The next plan was to keep the bulldozers out of the Park. There they were already, huddled in a menacing bunch outside the fence, along with a scraper, a ripper, an excavator and a dumper truck, all looking like monstrous beetles ready to crawl.

So Sir Marmaduke summoned the keepers to bring on the animals. Bunbo the elephant came first, followed by Hippo, Giraffe, Rhinoceros, Camel and Bison. They were the heaviest animals in the Safari Park, and they formed into a brave picket line to face the bulldozers.

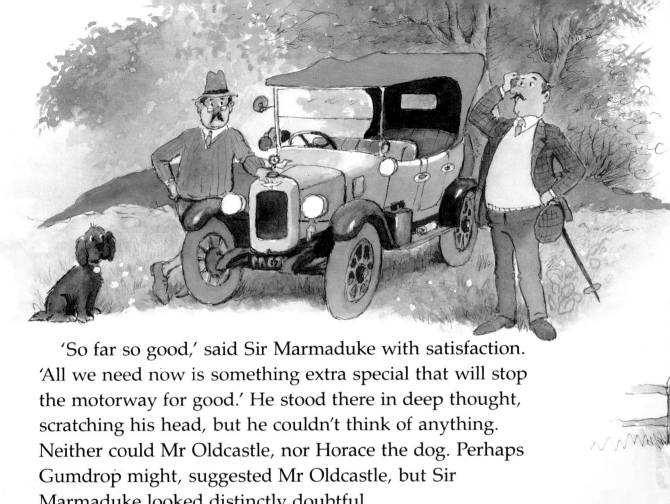

'So far so good,' said Sir Marmaduke with satisfaction. 'All we need now is something extra special that will stop the motorway for good.' He stood there in deep thought, scratching his head, but he couldn't think of anything. Neither could Mr Oldcastle, nor Horace the dog. Perhaps Gumdrop might, suggested Mr Oldcastle, but Sir Marmaduke looked distinctly doubtful.

Meanwhile there was work to do. Mr Oldcastle rolled up his sleeves and lowered Gumdrop's hood. For the next two days he drove out to the picket line with huge loads of food for the animals. There was hardly enough room for Horace, and the extra weight made Gumdrop's wheels sink deep into the soft ground.

On yet another trip Gumdrop carried such a heavy load that his back wheels sank right down and he got stuck. The wheels kept on spinning, churning up the ground in a muddy spray, but Gumdrop only sank deeper and deeper. Try as he may, Mr Oldcastle was quite unable to get the car out of the rut.

A keeper came to help.
'This is a job for the
elephant,' he said and off
he went to fetch a harness.
Bunbo the elephant was duly
hitched up and he pulled Gumdrop
out in a single mighty heave.
Mr Oldcastle looked at the ground where the spinning wheels
had churned it up. It was a deep rut all right – and there was
something glinting at the bottom of it. What on earth could it be?

'Horace!' he commanded. 'Dig, boy, dig!' The dog needed no encouragement, because he could smell a bone down there. He dug down so furiously that he disappeared in a shower of earth. When he emerged at last, he had a big bone in his mouth.

Mr Oldcastle looked down into what had by now become a great big hole – and stared. So did the keeper and Sir Marmaduke who had just arrived. For down that hole there seemed to be an ancient pot with some gleaming pieces scattered around it.

'Bunbo!' commanded Sir Marmaduke. 'See what's down there!' The elephant reached down with his long trunk and brought up a large pot. As he did so, a stream of coins poured out of it, straight into Sir Marmaduke's hands.

He goggled at them in astonishment and gasped. 'These are ancient Roman coins, by Jupiter! A veritable treasure trove!' Mr Oldcastle was so excited himself that his moustache quivered. Perhaps *this* could be that extra special thing they needed!

Sir Marmaduke replaced the coins in the pot and got out his portable phone. He rang his friend Professor Octavius Shard, the world-famous archaeologist. The Professor came over right away, with his team of expert diggers – and a television crew. (He was so famous that wherever he went, the television was sure to follow.)

The team got down to work without delay. They dug here, probed there, surveyed and measured everywhere, while the Professor made copious notes. When he finished he looked as if he might burst with excitement at any moment.

'This is big,' he choked straight into the cameras. 'There's not only a lot more treasure under here, but a large Roman Palace as well. What's more,' and he was shouting now, 'if we don't find a whole Roman town too, my name is not Octavius Shard!'

Sir Marmaduke said that he would be delighted if that were the case. 'Unfortunately,' he added, 'this site will be bulldozed on Monday for a new motorway.'

'Not if I can help it,' declared Mr Oldcastle gruffly, 'but there's no time to lose. Sir Marmaduke, please lend me the treasure trove, and the two petitions. Horace, fetch your Roman bone and get into Gumdrop. Professor, be so good as to follow my dog, because we are going on a trip.'

Professor Shard was rather unwilling to go at first, but when he saw that both the television cameras were still on him, he settled into Gumdrop, looking world-famous. Mr Oldcastle jumped in too, swung the car out of the park gates, down the road and up the motorway, all the way to London.

Never mind the noise or the traffic on the smelly motorway, he thought, this was important. And Gumdrop went faster than ever before in all his long life.

They arrived at the British Museum in record time. The experts there were so impressed by Gumdrop's treasure trove, the Professor's report, the long petitions and Horace's Roman bone that they decided to act at once. They jumped into Gumdrop there and then, and raced across town to tell the Government Minister right away. The camera crew followed and took pictures of everything.

That night the story was on television and the whole country waited to see what would happen next.

Monday came – and so did the bulldozers. They were ready to dig. Gumdrop was facing them on the picket line, with the heavy animals lined up behind him, all glaring angrily across the fence. Even Horace bared his teeth.

The chief engineer called across. 'For the last time, PLEASE remove those animals! My bulldozers must start digging right away.' All the while the cameras whirred to witness the battle to come. The tension was terrible.

'STOP!' yelled a commanding voice. It was the
Government Minister himself, who had just arrived in
Sir Marmaduke's Silver Ghost. When he saw the television
crew, he stood in front of the cameras, looking important.

'I have an announcement to make. Owing to a discovery
of treasure trove made by that splendid vintage car there,'
he said, pointing at Gumdrop, 'we have reason to believe
that there is a major Roman site under this ground, likely to
be the biggest discovery of the century. Because it needs
careful excavation and preservation, I have decided to build
this motorway somewhere else.'

A great cheer went up. Even the bulldozers hooted, because really they were glad to leave the Park in peace. As they turned to go away, the animals sent up a cheer of their own. Bunbo the elephant trumpeted, Bison bellowed, Hippo grunted, the others huffed or snorted, while Horace the dog barked fit to burst. As for Gumdrop, his klaxon went BLEEP BLEEP, and his brass horn gave a triumphant HONK!